Cover photo by Richard

i

THE RELUCTANT DETECTIVE

The Reluctant Detective

Calvin Hight Allen

Calvinz

MORE BY THE AUTHOR

JC Allen, DVM: Adventures in Veterinary Medicine

Zombie Co-Pilot and Other Bicycling Tales

Sammy

Red

CONTENTS

1 - The Unknown Caller 1

2 - Calling Into The Abyss 5

3 - Talking To A Dead Line 11

4 - Segueing Into The Law 14

5 - Go North, Young Man 20

6 - The Great White North 25

7 - Sparkbag 29

8 - Headed To Sparkbag 34

9 - Touring Ground Zero 38

10 - Pay Dirt 44

11 - Brent's Second Burial 50

DEDICATION

For Kimmel & Associates employees, especially the Heavy Civil hombres.

"[Recruiting] is a million-dollar experience, shoved up your ass one nickel at a time."

INTRODUCTION

Dan Weaver is an executive recruiter who specializes in heavy civil construction. One day, he gets a call from a young mother whose husband has disappeared in the oil-sands fields of Canada. Reluctant at first, Dan finds himself wondering about the young engineer's fate. Dan starts calling to locate the missing husband -- and is drawn into a mysterious case that leads him to play detective in the wilds of Canada.

PROLOGUE

Dan Weaver, said Dan.

Mr. Weaver, this is Bill Winslow, Midwestern Operations Manager for Flameco, said a brusque voice.

Good afternoon, said Dan.

I hear you have been trying to steal our employees, said Winslow, and we don't appreciate it.

No, you don't understand, said Dan.

I know what headhunters do, said Winslow. Quit calling Flameco employees. Now.

I'm not a headhunter, I'm a husband hunter, said Dan, but he was talking to a dead line. He slipped his headphones off and wondered. Why would a high-powered exec from one of the largest companies in the world care whether a headhunter was calling his co-workers? He wouldn't have time to care. Unless, thought Dan.

Unless one of his employees had disappeared -- and somebody was looking for him.

1

THE UNKNOWN CALLER

The Unknown Caller

The call came early.

Dan was sliding into his faux Naugahyde chair when Tonya's voice purred over the intercom. Danny Boy? she asked in her best predator voice.

Tonya, your voice is better than any cup of coffee, said Dan.

Danny, I've got a UK on the line, she said.

Why me, Tonya? I thought we were friends? Dan said.

She asked for you by name, Danny Boy, Tonya said.

She? Dan asked. Shes were rare.

She, Tonya said. What, so NOW you're interested?

Put her on, T Bone, Dan said.

Dan's phone chirped, and he put on his headphones, turned on his computer.

photo by Alena Darmel, Pexels

Dan Weaver here, he said.

Mr. Weaver? asked a voice. It really was a woman. My name is Edna Thomas. I hear you find people, is that right?

Dan slumped in his chair. He watched icons swim into view on his dark monitor. This was not a client. This was not a candidate. This was a clueless Unknown Caller.

Yes mam, Dan said. Well, sort of. I find professional executives for construction companies. A pause to let her think, to let her see that she had the wrong Dan Weaver.

Yes, yes, she said. I've heard what you usually do, Thomas said. But I'm calling to ask you to do a slightly different search.

We don't look for hourly employees, Dan said.

Mr. Weaver, if you'll just hear me out, Thomas said. My husband Brent was recruited by another headhunter six months ago to take a job in the oil fields in Canada. He had been out of work for a while, he's a mechanical engineer, and he really didn't want to go up north, but we needed the money. But they were in a big hurry to get him up there, so he flew up and started work, but now I can't find him anywhere.

When was Brent Thomas hired? Dan asked. And who hired him?

He was hired by a Canadian company named Flameco on June 15, 2016, Thomas said. He flew into Calgary on Air Canada Flight 3456, and we haven't heard from him since.

We? Dan asked.

Brent and I have two girls, she said. They really miss their daddy.

You mean he's not calling home? Dan asked.

2

No, I mean he's gone, she said. After he didn't call home for a week, I got worried and called the sheriff up there. They looked for Brent. They're saying he never made it to his new job, but he called me for two weeks after he got there, so I know that's not true. Her voice rose with fear.

Dan's computer was awake, and he was getting there. OK, hold on, he said. How long since you heard from your husband?

It's been two weeks now, she said, sobbing. The girls and I are worried sick. We haven't slept in days. I know this is not what you usually do, but I also heard you've got a wife and kids of your own, and that you were good at finding people. If you could help, I'll pay you double what you usually make.

I don't think you understand, m'am, Dan said. I'm not a detective, I'm a headhunter. I call people on the phone and tell them about jobs they might be interested in. I don't travel around the country looking for lost husbands.

She was crying hard now, dammit. This was the worst UK ever. Dan googled Canadian oil while he waited for her to wind down. The oil sands were right at the top: Boom towns.

photo by Samuel Walker, Pexels

No housing. Crowds of desperate men clumped together on the frozen wastelands. An easy place to disappear.

Mam? Dan asked.

Yes? she said, her voice composed now, hard.

Ms Thomas, I'll tell you what I'll do, Dan said. I'll make a few calls, see what I can find out about your husband, and get back to you. But probably you're going to end up with the sheriff again, or maybe the FBI if we're lucky. Can you email me some information about Brent?

They exchanged contact information and Dan poked his phone's red light. He clicked images on google, looked at photos of the oil sands: vast parking lots of heavy machinery, monster trucks rimed with ice. He clicked over to his customer database. It was time to get back to reality.

2

CALLING INTO
THE ABYSS

Late that afternoon, after all the money calls were done, Dan googled Edna Thomas. Her husband's name was Brent Thomas; their daughters were Isabel and Olivia. They looked to be a quiet Midwestern family, both parents from Michigan, degrees from Purdue, kids after five years of marriage.

Dan found Brent Thomas's resume on LinkedIn: internship with US Widget, three years on the road with building power plants until the first kid came along, then he moved to Bama Engineering six months ago.

Now lost in northern Bygod Canada.

~~~~~

Dan remembered one of his earlier placements who had figured out a way to lose himself. Dan had placed an estimator at a Charlotte site development company. After a few months, the company owner called Dan to ask for a replacement.

What happened? Dan asked.

You won't believe it, said the owner. We put Harold in his own office, gave him a company computer and vehicle, and a pile of blueprints to bid on. But he never showed us a bid -- or even part of one.

What?! Dan exclaimed.

It gets worse, the owner said. Harold started showing up for work with ladders strapped to his company vehicle.

Ladders! Dan said.

The owner chuckled. Finally, we looked at his computer, he said, and Harold was running a home-inspection business on our computer!

Are you serious? Dan asked.

Serious as a dead man lying in his coffin, said the owner. Nary a morsel of site estimating to be found. Of course, we fired Harold, and now we really need an estimator, what with being behind all those jobs he never bid.

I'll find you one ASAP for no fee, Dan had said.

Estimators had a reputation among headhunters for being squirrelly.

Dan remembered an estimator he placed with an Atlanta highway company. After a few months, Dan's client called and said, I don't think Jimmy's going to work out.

What's the problem? Dan asked.

The estimating department spent weeks putting together a $500-million bid on a giant interchange project, the client said. They even stayed up all night to put on some finishing touches. The bid was due at noon on a Friday, and they sent your guy in a company vehicle to deliver it. He was gone for hours, but when he returned, he still had the bid.

What?! Dan said.

I shit you not, said the client. He told us that he drove down to Atlanta and circled the building for an hour without finding a parking space -- so he came back without delivering the bid!

I'm so sorry, Dan said.

Of course we fired him on the spot, said the client. I hope you can find us a better estimator, and I thought you might want to know about this one.

Of course I'll find you a better one, Dan said, and at no charge to the company.

~~~~~~

Superintendents could be strange, too.

Dan remembered the time he recruited a superintendent for a site development company in Charleston, SC. It was early in Dan's career, and so he didn't ask about the man's height and weight -- a diplomatic way to weed out obese candidates.

After the interview, Dan called the client to see how it had gone.

Dan, have you ever met [the super]? his client asked.

No, Dan said.

I didn't think so, said his client.

Why do you ask? Dan said.

Well, he must weigh about 400 pounds, the client said. He got tired following me to our seats in the restaurant. In fact, he told us he was bringing his wife along, so we paid for two airline seats, but it turned out that he couldn't fit in one seat.

I am so sorry, Dan said. I'll repay y'all for the airline fees, and I'll be sure to screen candidates more carefully in the future.

~~~~~

Dan ran Brent Thomas through the company's online criminal background software: nothing much there, a speeding ticket during his senior year at Purdue.

Dan called his lawyer buddy and got Mr. Thomas checked out on Lexis: dead end.

Dan threw his feet up on his desk and asked the room: Hey, does anybody know how to find a disappeared guy in northern Canada?

7

Isn't that sort of redundant? asked Broc. If he's in northern Canada, he's already disappeared.

No, said Dan. I mean GONE from Canada. His wife says he hasn't called in for two weeks, and the local sheriff says the company has no record of him making it to work six weeks ago.

Taylor cackled. Uh oh, Dan's adopted a pretty widow lady, he said. How's she going to pay you Danny Boy?

Have some respect for the disappeared, said Dan.

He's probably buried in a shallow grave, said Mike. It's pretty wild up there in the boom-towns: no law, lots of drugs, thugs, and pugs.

Pugs, asked Billy?

Prostitutes, said Mike.

Why would you waste your time trying to find a guy lost in Canada? asked Dave. Does he work for a client?

Dan considered this. It was a damn good question. I tried to tell her no, he said.

Taylor was laughing again. When the poon calls, we must answer, he said.

Maybe run a search on companies working the boom, said Mike. We might have some guys up there you could talk to.

The hell with that, said Taylor. Google this widow lady to see if she's drink-worthy.

A couple calls came in, and the guys were back on the money calls. Dan ran a search on oil sands, and discovered that the field was huge, a giant underground reservoir that covered thousands of acres in Saskatchewan, Montana, and North Dakota. Great, he thought. Thomas could be anywhere. Dan researched the oil-sands boom online. Third largest supply in the world. Leases and wells springing up across the prairie. Once-dead crossroads converted into boom towns. Workers driving for hours from motel rooms, or crowded into "man-camps" sprawling barrack-like structures built by the oil companies and run like boot camps.

photo by Curioso Photography, Pexels

Dan ran a search of companies in the two states and scrolled through the list of employees. He called an office of Flameco, where Thomas was supposed to be working.

Flameco Williston, said a rough voice.

Dan Weaver for Brent Thomas, said Dan.

You said Thomas? the voice said.

Yes.

Hang on. A long silence. Dan googled Flameco while he waited. A multinational conglomerate that built all over the world, ran oilfields in Kuwait, hell, ran the Oval Office for a while, if these headlines were even half right.

No Brent Thomas here, buddy, said the rough voice.

Do you guys have any other offices in Canada? asked Dan, and felt foolish even as the words were leaving his mouth.

~~~~~

Blurting inappropriate words was fairly common in the headhunting world.

Dan remembered the young recruiter who had been working at Kimmel & Associates for a few months. He was given his first chance to qualify a candidate, and he started, as trained, by asking about the candidate's career goals. He asked about the candidate's family and feelings about moving.

When it was time to ask about the candidate's compensation package, the recruiter said, Let's talk about your package, and the associates within earshot burst into laughter. The recruiter's division honored him by naming its team "Let's talk about your package."

~~~~~

Rough voice was laughing at Dan's silly question. Only about a hundred, he said. Listen, I gotta go, good luck to you. He hung up and Dan listened to silence as he had for so many years.

Dan googled Flameco and got a list of 50 numbers. Oh, well, this he was good at. He started calling.

3

TALKING TO A
DEAD LINE

Over the next few days, Dan added Thomas calls to his money calls. On Thursday, he got a guy on the line who thought Brent Thomas's name "sounded familiar."

On Friday, Dan called Edna to check in. The hope in her voice made Dan feel like a fake.

No ma'm, not much to report yet, Dan said. Have you tried the FBI?

Yes, she said. They told me that they don't get involved unless there's a crime of some sort. I also contacted my congressman, but he hasn't called back.

Did your husband mention the names of any co-workers? asked Dan.

A pause, then, I don't remember, but I'll check my emails to see if he did, Edna said.

That's a good idea, said Dan. Can you forward me any correspondence you two had while he was up there? That might give me more names to call.

I will work on that, said Edna. Pause. How much do I owe you so far?

Nothing, said Dan. We don't get paid unless, I mean until, we find your husband.

Thank you so much, said Edna through a sob.

Dan clicked off and thought about not getting paid. It had been almost a month since he made his last deal, and he had almost forgotten what a paycheck looked like.

~~~~~

His chirping phone brought him out of his reverie, and Dan pulled on his headphones. I've got Bill Winslow with Flameco calling for you, said Tonya.

How slow is he, asked Dan?

Too slow to win, answered Tonya. She laughed. You're a nut, Danny Boy, you know that?

Not nutty, just too slow, said Dan. Let me talk to Mr. Win Slow.

Dan Weaver, said Dan.

Mr. Weaver, this is Bill Winslow, Midwestern Operations Manager for Flameco, said a brusque voice.

Good afternoon, said Dan.

I hear you have been trying to steal our employees, said Winslow, and we don't appreciate it.

No, you don't understand, said Dan.

I know what headhunters do, said Winslow. Quit calling Flameco employees. Now.

I'm not a headhunter, I'm a husband hunter, said Dan, but he was talking to a dead line.

Winslow didn't bother Dan at all. Over the years, Dan had grown used to threats from managers whose employees Dan had recruited.

~~~~~

Dan remembered recruiting a young project manager down in eastern North Carolina, only to realized the youngster had put Dan on speaker phone

An angry voice was suddenly on the line. You'd better stop recruiting my employees, or you'll be sorry, said the voice.

Just doing my job, Dan had said.

Yeah, well, if I catch you calling back here, I'm coming up to Asheville and cutting your balls off, the man had said.

Shaken, Dan had disconnected and told the story to the heavy-civil hombres.

If we don't get yelled at occasionally, we're not doing our job, Billy had said.

Tell that motherfucker that if he comes to Asheville, he'd better pack a lunch, Dave had said.

There's a reason you can't get into our office without buzzing the front desk, Mike had said.

~~~~~

Dan slipped his headphones off and wondered. Why would a high-powered exec from one of the largest companies in the world care whether a headhunter was calling his co-workers. He wouldn't have time to care. Unless, thought Dan.

Unless one of his employees had disappeared -- and somebody was looking for him.

4

SEGUEING INTO THE LAW

Over the weekend, Dan couldn't get the Thomases out of his mind. Transplanting lettuce in the garden, he would imagine the oily soil of Canada. Was Brent Thomas's body buried on the prairie? Riding his bike around the neighborhood, Dan thought about the Thomas kids, their toys idle while they studied their mother anxiously.

Dan was punching numbers early on Monday morning.

Altamont Police, said a woman.

Good morning, said Dan. This is Dan Weaver over at Kimmel and Associates. How are you doing this morning?

Well, Dan, it's Monday morning, said the voice. My name's Ginger Blevins, and that's about all I know this early. What can I do for you?

photo by Kindel Media, Pexels

I've got a friend whose husband disappeared in Canada, said Dan. How's the best way to go about getting the law involved?

I'd call the sheriff up there, and also call the CSIS.

CSIS? Dan asked.

The Canadian Security Intelligence Service, Ginger said. It's sort of like our FBI.

Also, get his name on the Canadian Police Information Center, said Ginger.

What's that? asked Dan.

It's a database where they list all wanted and missing and such, said Ginger. Anybody in law enforcement can pull it up if they find your friend's husband.

Thanks, Ms. Blevins, said Dan. I talked with the sheriff up there but he didn't seem very concerned. Any suggestions there?

Call me Ginger, honey, she said. I feel old enough on Monday morning without the miz; besides, I'm married with kids of my own. Do you know how many people go missing in North America? Happens all the time, and most of the time they end up in Vegas or some Godforsaken place married to a dancer. How long has he been gone?

Dan thought. About six weeks, he said. His wife's going crazy.

Lord, said Ginger. Do you have his full name and social? I can show you how they would put him in police information from here. And if you'll stop by the station, I can show you how I'd go about looking for him if he was my husband.

Dan agreed to stop by during Ginger's lunch hour with the Brent Thomas information. He extinguished the red eye on his phone with authority, and smiled at his new map of the oil-sands territory.

Finally, some good news for Edna.

~~~~~

Dan remembered another time that he was adopted by a friendly stranger. He had sent resumes of asphalt-paving managers to Sam Gibbs, the owner of a small site company, when Dan was a clueless rookie. One day, Dan caught Sam driving to a remote job site, and Sam had given Dan a crash course in heavy-civil construction.

After land is cleared, water and sewer pipes are laid underground, Sam had said. After those are in place, we build roads and any concrete structures, such as bridges, pump stations, retaining walls, that kind of thing. After the final grading, the asphalt paving and sidewalks are built. We sub out the asphalt and fine grading, so we won't be needing any asphalt managers, he had added gently.

Do y'all do highways? Dan had asked.

Sam chuckled. Not any more, he had said. I bid one early in my career and it nearly bankrupted the company. By the time I figured out that my project manager didn't know what he was doing, we were $300,000 in the red on the job. I fired him and hired an experienced super. We broke even on the job, and I learned how to build a highway, but we won't be doing any more any time soon.

Thanks for explaining all of that to me, Dan had said.

You're welcome, Sam had said. Keep us in mind for any seasoned site estimators.

You bet, Dan had said.

Sam had grown his company from $1 million per year into $25 million a year -- and Dan had been instrumental in helping. Eventually, Sam retired to build projects in Africa for his church. One of Sam's placements had become president and part owner of Sam's company.

~~~~~

Dan's phone chirped and Tonya said, Danny Boy?

Tonya Girl, said Danny.

Shoot, said Tonya. Can't remember his name, some guy from Bamalama.

Close enough, said Dan.

Hey, who was that woman called the other day, Tonya wanted to know.

Why T Bone, I do believe you're a little jealous, said Dan.

Well yes, said Tonya. Your wife and I don't want any more hussies muddying up the water.

She's a pore Momma who lost her hubby in Canada, said Dan.

Lost her hubby, said Tonya. Why'd she call you?

Hell, I don't know, said Dan. You're the one who put her through.

So now it's my fault, said Tonya. Just like a man. Here's Mr. Bamalama. And she was gone.

Dan Weaver, said Dan.

Dan, this is Rufus with Goodpave Construction down in Alabama.

Morning, Rufus, said Dan. How are you doing?

Well, not so good, Rufus said. That Equipment Manager you sent me got drunk last night and wrecked a company truck. He paused to let that sink in.

17

photo by Robert So, Pexels

I am so sorry to hear that, said Dan. Was he hurt? How bad is the truck?

Lucky for us, he's fine – but I fired him of course, Rufus said. The truck's not bad, still drivable. But I need another Equipment Manager quickly. You got any more in your back pocket?

I'll have to go back and look at my list, said Dan. I'm sure I can find you a better guy.

OK, make it fast, said Rufus. It's paving season, and we're balls to the walls.

I'm on it, said Dan. Thanks for giving Abraham a chance. I guess he fell off the wagon.

Yeah, said Rufus. More like he fell off my truck. The line went dead.

Dan punched the Red Eye and slumped. Shit, he said aloud.

That didn't sound good, said Mike.

Not good, agreed Dan. I've got to replace an Equipment Super for a little piss-ant company down in bum fuck, Alabama. My guy went on a bender and wrecked a company truck. He dug through a drawer and found the file folder for Goodpave Equipment Super: three names on the list, Abraham circled in red.

Ah, Alabama, said Taylor. Where men are men and sheep are nervous.

Anybody got any equipment guys who'll go down to the middle of Nowhere in the Deep South and work for collard greens? Dan asked the room.

You might try Bubba Wilson, used to be with Salient Construction, said Billy. He's getting pretty desperate.

Does he know anything about paving equipment? asked Dan.

Maybe, said Billy. He's old as dirt, says he can fix anything that rolls.

Thanks, Billy, said Dan. I will definitely call him.

Dan called Bubba and a dozen more potential candidates: Bubba had just found a new job and nobody else was interested once they heard it was Goodpave; the company did not have a good reputation.

At 11:45, an alarm popped up on Dan's screen: Ginger Blevins.

5

GO NORTH, YOUNG MAN

Dan stopped at a hot dog stand on his way to see Ginger Blevins. He listened to a jug band on the corner of Patton and Haywood while he wolfed his brat, dropping a dollar in the fiddle case.

photo by Elina Sazonova, Pexels

The Asheville police station was a light brick fortress that also housed the Fire Department. Dan went to the information desk and asked for Ginger Blevins. After a minute or so, a door opened, and a plump woman in a suit stuck her head out, waved him forward.

Ginger Blevins, she said, holding out a hand and giving him a warm smile.

Dan Weaver, he said. Her grip was firm.

Come on back, I'll show you a couple of detective short cuts, said Ginger.

Dan followed her through a warren of offices, into a smoked glass office with her name on the door. Two chairs sat in front of her desk, which was covered with stacks of paper.

I hope you don't mind if I eat while we talk, said Ginger.

Not at all, said Dan. I already ate, so I'll just take notes. He pulled out a legal pad from his pack and sat.

While she waited for her computer, Ginger unwrapped a sandwich from a used bread bag, took a big bite.

~~~~~

While he waited for Detective Blevins, Dan remembered marketing Keith, a highly skilled asphalt paving manager to clients in the Southeast. Having managed an entire company doing $20 million per year, Keith was earning about $200,000 per year.

One of the companies who had an interest was a family-owned paving company in the panhandle of Florida. They flew Keith down to Jacksonville on a Friday, and he spent the whole weekend with them.

When Dan called on the following Monday to ask how it had gone, Keith said, That's one of the wildest job interviews I've ever been on.

The company drove him all over the panhandle, showing him about $50 million worth of operations. They introduced him to the executive team, and discussed the company's plans for expansion.

Saturday night is when it really got interesting, Keith said. They asked me if I liked hunting dogs, and I said, Sure. We drove out in the woods to a hunting club and loaded up a few cars with dogs. We drove into the woods, built a fire, and released the dogs. Next thing I knew, a jar of moonshine was being passed around, and somebody was cooking up a big rack of ribs. We listened to the dogs hunt most of the night, and just before dawn, the CEO said, Keith, we really like you, and we feel like you'd do a good job at our company. We want to offer you $75,000 per year plus a company vehicle and a chance for unlimited bonuses -- What do you say?

I kept my face straight and told them just what you had recommended -- Fellows, I'm honored to get your offer. I need to talk it over with my wife, and I'll get back with you within 24 hours.

On the other end of the spectrum, Dan's client that actually hired Keith offered a compensation package that included: a career path that showed Keith how he could end up running the company's entire Southeast operations (about $500 million worth); $150,000 salary (the highest the corporation allowed); a guaranteed bonus for five years of $50,000, followed by unlimited bonuses geared to the division's profits; a company vehicle PLUS a generous vehicle allowance, effectively adding $10,000 to the package; five years worth of per diem (even though Keith wouldn't be traveling much); company-paid health insurance PLUS covering his out-of-pocket deductibles for five years; a moving package worth $10,000; and other minor perks such as country club memberships and tuition payments.

~~~~~

OK, I'm ready, Blevins said.

Dan told her everything he knew about the Thomases and everything he had found out on the telephone, including the strange call from Flameco.

Ginger entered Brent Thomas into NCIS, and sent a bulletin to Canadian law enforcement using the description from the photo his wife had sent Dan.

Now, when you get up there, check in with local law enforcement, said Ginger. She held the back of her hand to her mouth while she chewed. You want all their numbers plugged into your cell phone.

I was hoping not to go up there, said Dan. Can't we get an officer up there to look around?

Ginger was shaking her head. I'm telling you, missings are way down the list in terms of priority, she said. You might get a couple of leads on the phone, but if you really want to find Mr. Thomas, you're gonna have to go up there and do the work.

But I don't even know what work to do, said Dan. I'm a headhunter, not a detective.

Tell you what, said Ginger, picking a grape from a Tupperware. This Thomas family sounds like good people. Do what you can from here, maybe you'll get lucky. But if you have to go up there, you can call me and I'll lead you through it.

Are you a travel agent or a detective? said Dan. I've got my own family here, my own garden to weed. Are you going to plant my beans for me?

Ginger smiled. I'm not saying you should go, she said. You're the one who adopted these people. I'm just offering to help – from here. She pushed a legal pad with a list of numbers across the desk. Here's your Detective Starter Kit. Call me when you're on the ground in Canada. And take lots of pictures, I love a good picture.

On his way back to work, Dan called his wife Mary. He told her about his meeting with Ginger.

You're not going to Canada, said Mary. It was not a question.

I'm hoping to avoid it, said Dan. But Ginger says somebody will probably have to go to find out what happened to Brent Thomas.

But not you, said Mary.

Let's talk when I get home, said Dan.

Talk doesn't pay the bills, said Mary.
It does when I talk, said Dan.

6

THE GREAT WHITE NORTH

After assuring Mary that he would only be gone for a few weeks, tops, and that he'd earn more during those weeks than he had all year at Kimmel & Associates, Dan got a job with Flameco as an internal recruiter in the regional office at Fort McMurray.

After he got settled into his room, Dan called Ginger Blevins, the Asheville detective.

What should I do first? Dan asked.

Have you contacted local law enforcement? Blevins asked.

Yep, they asked me to keep them informed, said Dan.

OK, the next thing to do is discreetly identify Flameco employees who like to talk, Blevins said. Human sources are the best.

After talking with Blevins for 30 minutes, Dan had a plan.

Two weeks later, Dan walked into the Human Resources office, wearing a Kimmel & Associates hardhat. He followed a young woman into an office, where a crew-cut man was staring at a computer screen.

photo by Andra Piacquadio, Pexels

Welcome to Flameco, said the man, rising to shake Dan's hand. I'm HR Manager Arnie Jones. Tell me again why you're here?

I'm your new internal recruiter, said Dan. Flameco wants me to recruit employees, young engineers in particular.

Yeah, I remember now, said Jones.

My assistant will show you to your office. Get settled in, and then call me. I've got a list of job sites and the employees we need for you.

It didn't take Dan long to settle into his new job at Flameco.

~~~~~

It was much easier than his first few months at Kimmel & Associates. Kimmel had put Dan and five other newbies in the pit -- a windowless cube farm deep in the bowels of the building. The pit boss was an oily former headhunter named Butcher. Butcher gave all the rookies a legal pad to go with their phones.

Call all the companies in your territory, Butcher had said. Ask for the chief estimator, and try to find out what jobs their company are building or bidding. Also, ask the chief what their career goals are.

Dan went with two other heavy civil rookies to the public library, where they printed off the names of all the heavy civil companies they could find. Back in his cube, Dan called every swimming-pool company in Florida and asked the receptionist,

Do y'all build highway? He made 108 calls the first day, and got no further than the receptionist.

His second day, Dan had gotten a division president of a giant civil company on the phone to ask what his division might need.

If you find a superstar, let me know, the manager had said.

Elated, Dan had written superstar on a Kimmel job-order form and sprinted into Butcher's office.

I just got a job order, Dan had said.

Tell me, Butcher had said.

Dan had passed the job-order form over to Butcher, who tossed it into the trash. That's not a job order, that's a blow-off line, he had said. Get back on the phone.

~~~~~

At Flameco, Dan chatted up folks in the break room and zeroed in on Sam Dinwiddie, a computer geek in the HR Department. As a bespectacled nerd, Sam was a loner, and eager to see Dan as a possible friend. The two men started taking breaks together, and Dan learned that Sam had left a wife behind, just like Dan.

After a few lunches together, Dan probed to see if Sam would look up Thomas.

Why do you need his number? asked Sam. I'm not supposed to give out information to anyone except kin and supervisors.

Tom and I went to school together, said Dan. I just heard from my wife, who is friends with Tom's wife, that he works for Flameco somewhere in the oil sands.

Why don't you get Tom's number from his wife? asked Sam.

I tried that already, said Dan, but she can't reach him, either. The number he gave her is not in service.

Sam sighed. He looked around the cafeteria. I'm giving you this one number only, he said. If it's wrong, or out of service, you're on your own.

Dan held up both hands. That's great, he said. Can you make it his cell phone?

The next day, Sam slid a scrap of paper across the table to Dan. Here's Brent Thomas's cell number, he said.

Dan folded the paper and slipped it into his pocket. Sam, you're the man! he said.

That night, back in his room, Dan called Brent Thomas's company cell number -- out of service. At least I know he worked for Flameco, Dan said to the empty room.

7

SPARKBAG

Based on Brent Thomas's cell number, Dan narrowed his search to four job sites north of Fort McMurray. Between his Flameco calls, mostly to universities to set up career fairs, he called numbers at the Millenium job site. After talking with a couple hundred Flameco workers there, none of whom had heard of Brent Thomas, he moved on to the MacKay River job site. Meanwhile, he continued to eat lunch with Sam, keeping the acquaintance warm in case Dan might need more information.

Every Saturday, Dan called Brent's wife Edna to report on his progress -- or lack of progress. Trying to sound brave, she alternated between gratitude and strength.

Asheville Detective Ginger Blevins kept encouraging Dan.

You're turning into a fine detective, she said. You're doing exactly what I would be doing -- if I were undercover.

On Fridays, Dan called Taylor Moreland, a Kimmel co-worker who had agreed to keep an eye on Dan's Kimmel work while Dan was "gallivanting," as Taylor put it. One Friday, Taylor was excited to report that he had made a deal with one of Dan's clients.

Hey, I just placed a Projecto Managerio with Homestead Contracting down in south Florida, Taylor said. He's bilingual and fluent in P3. I hope you'll give me a good cut of the deal.

How does 75% sound? Dan asked.

Awesome, Taylor said. I'll hand in a pink sheet.

Don't hand it in until the managerio has been on the job for a week, Dan said. You know that's my rule -- I hate green sheets.

OK, Taylor said. By the way, how's your search going for the missing husband?

It reminds me of executive search, Dan said. A lot of phone calls with no results.

Well, hurry back, Taylor said. The Heavy Civil guys all miss you. Hey guys, I've got Dan on the phone!

Get your ass back down here! We bolted plastic bull balls to your chair! Voices shouted in the background.

Dan smiled. It was nice to be missed. OK, gotta go, he said. Thanks, Taylor.

After dozens of calls to MacKay River employees, Dan called another young engineer who remembered Brent Thomas.

photo by Anamul Rezwan, Pexels

Yeah, I know him, said Paul Binion. We worked together at Kiewit, and he used to be on this job.

Great, said Dan. Any idea where he's working now?

No idea, said Paul. I haven't talked to him in weeks. I'm pretty sure he's not at

MacKay River. You might try Fort Hills.

Fort Hills? asked Dan.

Yeah, said Paul. It's the northernmost job site, supposedly the coldest, too.

~~~~~

Talking to Paul reminded Dan of Horace, a young Canadian engineer he had placed with a small bridge contractor in south Florida. Zohan Zap, the owner of the company, was one of Dan's favorite owners to talk to. Although Dan placed only Horace at Zap Contracting, Dan loved to talk with Zap. Zap had emigrated from eastern Europe as a young man, graduated from engineering school, and started his own company at an early age.

I need a flunky, Zap had said one day.

A flunky? Dan had asked.

Yes, Zap had said. I'm bidding a Corps of Engineering job, and I have to send in the resume of a quality control guy. At Zap, we do quality control as part of our other jobs, but the Corps wants a flunky. It's no wonder government jobs cost more to build.

OK, Dan had said. I'll find you a flunky.

Don't waste your time, Zap had said. I would never pay a fee for a flunky. I just thought you might find it funny.

When Dan had sent Horace's resume, Zap had said, I think we just might make something out of this one.

Twenty years later, Horace was a part owner, and in line to take over the company when Zap retired.

~~~~~

At Flameco, Dan dialed into the automated phone system at Fort Hills, and discovered dozens more names to contact. Working methodically, he started with Jim Allen and worked his way toward Linda Zott.

After he set up another career fair at the University of Lethbridge, Dan punched in another number at the Fort Hills job site.

Fort Hills, Isaac speaking, said a young-sounding voice.

Dan Weaver for Brent Thomas, said Dan.

Hmm, said Isaac. I haven't heard that name before, but I've only been here a week. Hold on.

The phone went dead for a while, and Dan thought he might have gotten disconnected. Are you still there? said the voice.

Still here, said Dan.

Brent Thomas is no longer at this job site, said Isaac. Nobody knows where he might be.

Did he leave a number? asked Dan.

Nope, said Isaac.

Thanks anyway, said Dan. He hung up the phone and looked at his map of Flameco's job sites. There was only one left -- Sparkbag.

What the hell was a sparkbag?

On the Flameco web site, he learned that First Nation tribe members carried the embers of one fire to other campsites in sparkbags, which saved the aborigines from having to start a new fire.

photo by Jimmy Chan, Pexels

Just as the sparkbag was innovative for its time, Flameco's techniques for removing and refining oil from sands is innovative now, read the web site.

I wonder whether Brent Thomas got burned at Sparkbag? thought Dan.

8

HEADED TO SPARKBAG

Dan and Sam Dinwiddie were eating lunch in the Flameco cafeteria at Fort McMurray. Sam was picking the raw onions out of a Greek salad, and Dan was working on a burger.

What do you know about Sparkbag? Dan asked Sam.

Sparkbag the job site? responded Sam.

Dan nodded, chewing.

It's a whopper, said Sam. Probably the biggest site we've got. And the most dangerous.

Dangerous? asked Dan.

Sam nodded. The hydrocracker, he said. Anytime you're using hydrogen to refine oil, there's the possibility of an accident.

Have you ever heard of anyone getting killed at Sparkbag? asked Dan.

Sam studied Dan across the table. For a recruiter, you sure do ask some strange questions, Sam said.

Dan shrugged. You said it was dangerous, he said. I just wondered how dangerous it was.

Sam chewed, thinking. I know that, at one of Flameco's competitor's refineries, there was an explosion, killing one worker and injuring others, he said. But that's unusual; I heard the company didn't follow safety guidelines.

That night, Dan researched hydrocracking on the internet. A lot of it was over his head, but he zeroed in on the hydro-cracker as the most dangerous place at the Sparkbag job site. During the refining process, explosions and fires could occur if pipes failed -- and pipes sometimes failed, Dan knew.

photo by Kateryna Babaieva, Pexels

If Brent Thomas was killed in an industrial accident in the wilds of Canada, would the company report it -- or would they hide the body and hope for the best?

That night, when he called home, Mary sounded concerned. The money

has been great, she said, but I'm worried about you being at such a remote location.

I'm at the regional headquarters, said Dan. It's the equivalent of a mid-sized city, with lots of people around. I'm just sitting in an office, same as I was back at home. Besides, I'm nearly finished up here, I think -- I'll be home before you know it.

Just promise me you'll be careful, she said.

I promise, Dan said.

The next morning, Dan started zeroing in on Brent Thomas -- if the young man had indeed worked at the Sparkbag site.

First, he started researching the Sparkbag site, so that he could recruit new workers for the site. The Sparkbag site turned out to be the company's largest, with its own private airport, housing, rec centers, and cafeteria. Hundreds of workers lived, worked, played, and shopped at the site.

The company mined oil from the sands beneath the site. First, two wells were drilled side by side to the layer of sand (called bitumen) that contained oil . Next, the wells were drilled horizontally for a kilometer through the bitumen; the wells were about 30 feet apart. Next, high pressure steam was pumped to the upper well, which had holes to release the steam into the bitumen. The steam melted the bitumen, which drained down into the lower well. The mixture of bitumen and water was pumped to the surface and over to a refinery.

At the refinery, the slurry was piped to a hydrocracker, which combined the slurry with hydrogen to crack the heavy slurry molecules into gasoline and other distillates. The resulting mixture was refined into jet fuel, diesel, and other products.

photo by James Frid, Pexels

Dan got sleepy as he read the technical descriptions, but one thing was clear -- hydrocracking could be dangerous -- the Canadian Centre for Occupational Health and Safety (CCOHS) had reported several workers killed in hydrocracking explosions.

After he understood hydrocracking's dangers, Dan started calling everyone at the Sparkbag job site, hoping to find someone who knew Thomas, or even better, to find Thomas himself. Dan methodically worked his way through the Sparkbag phone directory. Thomas wasn't listed in the directory -- he had either been transferred or buried under the frozen tundra.

After dozens of calls, Dan finally

spoke with Emmett Allen, another young engineer who re-membered Thomas.

Yeah, I remember Thomas, Allen said. (Was it Dan's imag-ination, or did Allen lower his voice?) Why do you want to speak with him?

Just routine personnel questions, Dan said, trying to keep his voice light.

I haven't seen Thomas in, oh, weeks, said Allen. (His voice was definitely lowered.) It's odd, too, because he and I were friends, and the company won't tell me where he went. If you find him, ask him to call me.

Will do, Dan said. He hung up and sighed. He was headed to Sparkbag.

9

TOURING GROUND ZERO

It was easy for Dan to get permission to travel to the Spark-bag site. Because Sparkbag was so remote, the company was desperate for more workers there, and sending an internal recruiter there to learn more about the site made perfect sense.

Dan flew on a company jet and landed at a company airport. Picked up in a company bus, he checked into company housing, which was almost luxurious.

The next morning, Dan walked over to the administration building to get permission to tour the site. He was directed to the superintendent's office, a burly redheaded man named Jarrett Smith. Smith was not happy to see Dan.

I don't understand why a recruiter needs to tour my job site, Smith said. You can get all the information you need off the company website.

Dan tried to appear nonchalant. I'm with you, sir, but the company wants me to learn the refining process top to bottom, he said.

Smith sat back in his chair and blew out a loud breath. OK, he said, but here's the way it's gonna be: no snooping around on your own -- I want you to be with one of my guys all the time -- are we clear?

Yes sir, Dan said. With one of your guys all the time.

You'll start with the hydrocracker, Smith said. It's the heart of the operation. He pushed a button on his cell phone. Sawyer? he barked. It's me. I need you to lead a recruiter on a tour of the 'cracker. Smith hung up. Wait in the lobby. John Sawyer will be your guide.

Dan stood up. Thanks, he said.

Smith shook his head. You're not welcome, he said. Do what Sawyer says.

Yes sir, Dan said. He sat in the lobby and read Petroleum Digest until a huge man in bib overalls showed up.

You the recruiter? the man asked.

Dan stood. Yes sir, he said, extending his hand. I'm Dan Weaver.

John Sawyer, said the man, ignoring Dan's hand. Let's get this over with. Follow me, and stay close.

Yes sir, Dan said.

The two men walked through the snow toward a tower of steaming pipes. Dan's boots crunched in the snow and his breath steamed in the cold.

photo by Orlando Schwarz, Pexels

How many hydrocrackers are on site? Dan asked.

One, Sawyer grunted.

Are we going there first? Dan asked.

Sawyer nodded, and kept walking.

They entered through a metal door at the base of the tower. Inside, a huge metal cylinder with pipes at the top and sides loomed over the men. Men in hard hats walked about the tower, checking dials.

Is this where hydrogen and the oil slurry are mixed? Dan asked.

Yup, Sawyer said. That's the 'cracker.

Dan walked around the tower, admiring its sleek lines. Do you have an

engineer on site? he asked. I'm focused on recruiting engineers right now.

Sawyer thought. Come on, he said.

They walked past two smaller towers to an office at the end of the building. Dan followed Sawyer into the office to a door with a name tag reading Albert Kiewit. Sawyer knocked on the door, and a voice said, Come in.

Sawyer and Dan went into the office, where a short, wire-haired man sat at a desk covered with papers.

Sawyer said, This here's a recruiter. He wants to talk with an engineer.

Kiewit stood up and extended his hand. I'm Al Kiewit, he said. Have a seat, and I'll be with you in a minute.

photo by Andrea Piacquadio, Pexels

I'll be right outside, said Sawyer. Don't wander off.

I won't, Dan said. He sat in a metal chair and picked up a Hydrocracking Journal.

Kiewit made a few notes, stacked some papers, and looked over at Dan.

How can I help you? Kiewit asked.

I'm an internal recruiter, said Dan. I'd like to talk with some of the engineers at Sparkbag to see what it's like to work here. That may help me recruit more folks to the company.

Kiewit nodded. Well, I can help you with that, he said. This facility is an engineering marvel. We take extremely low-grade oil-slurry, coming into our refinery mixed with all sorts of junk, and create high-quality petroleum products.

Dan jotted some notes. I've read that hydrocracking can be dangerous, he said. What do I tell prospects who're concerned about that?

Kiewit smiled. The industry has been hydrocracking for decades, he said. We've had only a few accidents, and those were due to sloppy maintenance or operations.

Thanks, Dan said. That's helpful. Are there any young engineers on the Sparkbag site I can talk to?

Kiewit frowned. How will that help the company? he asked.

We're trying to find young engineers, Dan said. They are cheaper to hire and can grow into tremendous assets. The problem is, a lot of them don't want to be working so remotely, where there's not much social life.

Kiewit stood and grabbed his jacket. Come with me, he said. I think we can find you a young engineer or two.

As the two men left Kiewit's office, Sawyer glared at Dan. Where are you taking this jackass? Sawyer demanded.

Relax, Kiewit said. He's harmless, and I'll be right with him the whole time.

Dan and Kiewit walked through the giant hydrocracking facility, past two more metals towers connected to the reactor by pipes.

Those are the separator and the fractionator, Kiewit said. By the time it comes out of the fractionator, it's a high-grade petro.

Dan nodded. Impressive, he said.

Kiewit found an engineer holding a clipboard and studying some gauges on the side of the separator. He tapped the young man on the shoulder.

photo by Antoni Shkraba, Pexels

Cal, this is Dan Weaver. He's an internal recruiter and I want you to help him. Walk him back to my office when y'all are finished. Dan, meet Cal Allen.

Yes sir, Allen said. He turned to Dan as Kiewit walked off. How can I help you?

What would attract a young engineer to the Sparkbag site? Dan asked.

Allen said, Let's walk while we talk. I've got to finish checking these gauges. From an engineering standpoint, hydrocracking is state-of-the-art, he said. The goo that we get from oil sands is a long way from usable, but 'cracking not only refines it into high-grade petro, it produces excess electricity and hydrogen.

Dan jotted in his notebook. What about a social life, he asked. If a young engineer is married with kids, and he gets stuck out here in the Canadian wilderness, won't he be lonely?

Allen nodded. Some do get lonely, he said. But the company facilities have a lot to offer: movies, games, bowling, swimming, a gym.

Dan wrote a note. Do you know a young engineer at Sparkbag named Brent Thomas? he asked.

Wasn't he the guy burned in the ... Allen said. Wait a minute, why are you asking about him?

Dan waved his hand dismissively. I heard he's another articulate young engineer I should talk to, he said.

Allen shook his head. Brent disappeared after that accident, he said. We were told he got air-lifted to a hospital in Saskatchewan, but I never heard a 'copter take off that day. He shrugged. Must've caught a flight out on a company jet -- I haven't seen him for weeks now.

10

PAY DIRT

Back in his office at Sparkbag, Dan thought about what he had learned. Brent Thomas had indeed been involved in an accident at Sparkbag -- but he had NOT caught a flight out.

He had disappeared.

Dan called the Flameco corporate headquarters in Calgary and asked for Human Resources. When he inquired about Thomas, he was told that the engineer still worked at the Sparkbag site.

What's his cell number? Dan asked.

I'm sorry, but I can't give out that information, said the personnel worker.

How about his job-site number? Dan asked.

Of course, she said. Hold for that number.

However, that number turned out to be the main Sparkbag number.

Dan knew from his earlier research that the risk of explosion in hydrocracking occurred only at the reactor itself, where tremendous heat and hydrogen made the process volatile. So he needed to talk with employees who were working the Sparkbag reactor the week that Brent went missing six weeks ago. Dan studied the Sparkbag names he had already: Superintendent

Jarrett Smith, Foreman John Sawyer, Senior Project Engineer Al Kiewit, and Project Engineer Cal Allen. He called Allen's cell number.

Allen here, Allen said.

Cal, it's Dan Weaver from recruiting, Dan said. I thought of follow-up questions.

Fire away, but make it fast, Allen said.

Do you know any young engineers who work around the reactor? Dan asked.

Silence.

They haven't replaced Thomas, and he was the only engineer at that location, Allen said.

What about other employees who work the reactor? Dan asked.

Let's see, Allen said. The foreman is a guy named Sawyer, and the mechanic is Jerry Wiseman.

Thanks, Dan said. I really appreciate it.

Dan left three messages for Wiseman on his office extension, but the mechanic didn't call back. Dan called every area office at Sparkbag, asking for Wiseman's cell. After a dozen calls, he was patched through.

Wiseman, Wiseman said curtly.

Mr. Wiseman, I'm a Flameco recruiter working to sign up folks to work at Sparkbag, San said.

So? Wiseman said.

I was told you were a good man to talk to about the reactor, Dan said.

What do you want to know? Wiseman asked.

How long have you worked for Flameco? Dan asked.

Twenty-five years, Wiseman said.

Why is it a good company to work for? Dan asked.

You know, the usual, Wiseman said. Good pay, benefits.

What about safety? Dan asked. Do you feel safe around the reactor?

Long's you follow the guidelines, you're ok, Wiseman said.

OK, thanks, Dan said. You've been a big help. Can you tell me how to get in touch with Brent Thomas?

A long silence.

Listen, said Wiseman. I can't talk about Brent over the phone.

The two men agreed to meet the next afternoon at the Sparkbag parking lot. Dan waited in his car until he saw a bearded man with a green hard hat walking toward a blue Jeep. Dan got out and met the man beside the Jeep.

You Wiseman? Dan asked.

Yep, Wiseman said. Get in. He pressed a button in his hand, and the passenger door unlocked. Wiseman drove to the middle of a crowded parking lot and let the car idle. He checked the nearby cars, his rear-view mirrors.

The only reason I'm sticking my neck out is because Brent was a good friend, he said. You've got to swear that you're on the level.

Listen, said Dan. The only reason I'm risking MY neck is because Brent's wife got to me -- she's hurting real bad and I want to help her. I'm not trying to be a hero, and I don't want Flameco to find out any more than you do.

OK, Wiseman said. Here's what I know. I'm only saying it once, and I don't want to hear from you again, got it?

Dan nodded.

Brent and I were working the 'cracker the night it blew, Wiseman said. I was lucky because I was down at the fraction-ator, but he was right in front of the main reactor gauge. I had been warning the company for weeks that that gauge needed replacing, but you've got to shut down the whole process to replace it, and they were set on hitting their production targets, so they hoped for the best.

Wiseman paused, blew out a deep breath.

Instead, they got the worst, he said, or rather Brent got the worst. When the gauge blew, it opened a three-foot crack in the reactor wall, and blasted Brent with burning oil sands and chemicals -- he never stood a chance.

You mean he's dead?! Dan said.

Hell yeah, dead, said Wiseman. Melted to a puddle by the time I got down there.

photo by Bence Szemerey, Pexels

We cut the juice to the reactor, but the fire was so hot that -- even after foaming it down -- we couldn't get close to Brent until he was almost entirely gone.

What did they do with his remains? Dan asked.

Wiseman shook his head sadly. I don't know, he said. They gave everybody on that shift the rest of the day off, made us swear that we'd keep it secret -- some bullshit about their CanOSH rating or something -- and that was that. They repaired the reactor in no time -- gotta keep that petro flowing. There was bitterness in his voice. I don't see what you or I can do at this point. He sat back in his seat, checked his surroundings again.

Who would have been in charge of clean-up? Dan asked.

Wiseman said, Maintenance, I guess.

Who's in charge of Maintenance? Dan asked.

That's Arnie Blevins, said Wiseman. Come to think of it, he might be a good one to talk with. I heard that he was not happy about cleaning up human remains.

What's his cell number? Dan asked. He saved Blevins's info in his phone. Why didn't the cops get involved?

Wiseman shook his head. You gotta understand the situation out here, he said. There are thousands of workers, they come and go all the time, and there's not much law enforcement. What few cops there are know how important oil sands are to their economy, so they tend to look the other way unless they're forced not to. He cranked the car and drove back to Dan's vehicle.

Good luck, Wiseman said. You're going to need it.

When Dan called Chief Mechanic Blevins later that day, the supervisor was wary.

I knew you or someone like you would be calling me about this one day, Blevins said. And you're in luck, because I've got a conscience. I put what looked like human remains into a plastic bag and stowed it behind the main garbage chute, over in building 13.

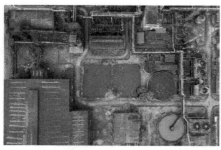

photo by Pok Rie, Pexels

That's all the help you're going to get from me -- lose my number and delete this call. He hung up.

Dan ended the call and took a deep breath. If he could get those remains to the cops -- and then to Edna Thomas -- maybe he could sleep easier.

If, he thought.

The next morning, Dan went to his office and grabbed his interview materials plus a large mail pouch. He walked out the back door and went behind the buildings to the entrance to Building 13. He looked around, then went into the building, which was a clearinghouse for waste for the whole site. The main chute was obvious -- it took up nearly the whole back wall.

photo by Matheus Bertelli, Pexels

Workers on skid steers zipped about the floor of the building. Dodging the four-wheel crafts, Dan walked to the main chute and pretended to consult his clipboard while he scanned the building for suspicious eyes. He waited until everyone's back was to him, then darted behind the chute. Under a pile of dusty cardboard, Dan found a plastic bag filled with dirt. He quickly stuffed it into his pouch and scuttled to the edge of the chute. When no one was looking, he walked back across the floor and out of the building.

11

BRENT'S SECOND BURIAL

In his room that evening, Dan opened the plastic bag with Thomas's remains. It was mostly ash with some lumps that could be bone. He resealed the bag and hid it in the return duct of his HVAC system.

The next day, Dan gave his two-week notice to Flameco, saying that he had grown homesick and that he would recruit his replacement if the company wanted him to.

Actually, you lasted longer than I thought you would, said Arnie Jones, the HR manager who had greeted Dan weeks ago. I thought you would have been already fired for snooping around about Brent Thomas.

Dan's heart started beating harder. What do you mean? he asked.

Why have you been asking about an employee who left the company weeks ago? Blevins asked.

Thomas is a young engineer, and I was hired to recruit young engineers, Dan said. I talked to every young engineer I could find at Flameco. I didn't know he had left until just recently.

Blevins slid a form across his desk. Be that as it may, I want you to sign this nondisclosure agreement, he said.

I'll be glad to, Dan said. He read over the form, which was written to protect company trade secrets, and signed it.

Blevins filed the form and stared at Dan. In light of your suspicious activity, I want you on the first flight out of here, he said, and slid a ticket over to Dan. Be ready to go at seven am tomorrow.

Yes sir, Dan said. Thanks for the chance to work at Flameco.

That night, he packed Thomas's remains in the middle of his checked luggage. As cheap insurance, he used his personal laptop to write up his findings, addressed it to the FBI office in Asheville, and set it to send in 24 hours.

The next morning, he got to the air terminal an hour early, and sat by his luggage reading a Hydrocracking Digest.

Dan Weaver, please report to security, a voice boomed over the loudspeaker.

Directed to security by customer service, he walked into a room to find a masked and gloved worker holding the duffle bag with Thomas's remains.

photo by Lucas Andreatta, Pexels

What the hell is this? the worker demanded.

My son is a geology buff, Dan said. I promised to bring him some oil sands.

You do realize, sir, that oil sands are well below the surface? the worker asked.

Dan nodded. He won't know the difference, he said. He's only 11.

The worker laughed. I guess you're right, he said. Have a good flight.

With sweat trickling down his sides, Dan repacked his suitcase and boarded his flight out of Canada. When he landed in Chicago, he called his wife to let her know he would be home early.

Oh, I'm so relieved, Mary said. I thought you might never make it back.

Wait til you hear the story, thought Dan.

He called Edna Thomas and gave her the news. She wept into the phone. I knew he was gone, she said. But at least I have something to bury.

The next day, Dan carried Thomas's remains to the local FBI office. After he told his story, the agent sat back in his chair. You realize how far-fetched this sounds, don't you, Mr. Weaver?

I understand, Dan said. But if you check these remains for DNA, I think you'll find some of Brent Thomas there.

We'll be in touch, the agent said.

So Dan went back to his job at Kimmel and waited. Months later, he found himself in a federal courtroom in Asheville,

photo by Sora Shimazaki, Pexels

testifying in a civil suit about his journey to Canada and his recovery of Thomas's remains. After weeks of testimony, the company settled for $10 million, payable to Thomas's widow and children.

At Brent Thomas's funeral,

photo by Rodnae Productions, Pexels

Dan stood beside Edna and her two children while the preacher said, ashes to ashes, dust to dust.

If you only knew, thought Dan.

The End

EPILOGUE

Dan Weaver retired from Kimmel & Associates and became a part-time detective in Asheville, NC. He specializes in missing persons cases.

Edna Thomas remarried and lives happily in Indiana.

The Heavy Civil Division is still going strong.

AUTHOR'S BIOGRAPHY

Calvin Hight Allen is a retired headhunter living in western North Carolina.

ACKNOWLEDGEMENTS

Thanks to the photographers at Pexels.

CPSIA information can be obtained
at www.ICGtesting.com
Printed in the USA
BVHW052058170323
660681BV00007B/105